JUST OUR TONY

ILLUSTRATIONS BY REBECCA BENDER

MAUREEN ROSE WILKIE

DEDICATION:

For my mom and dad who instilled a love of all animals in us three girls.

For Tony's human dad (Cory) and two human brothers (Dane and Brier) who love him immensely.

For Tony, who I realize came into my life when I needed him more than he needed me.

OUR TONY:

Our Tony is a handsome cat
A Tabby we are sure
With eyes of green and coat of brown
He talks and sings in purr!

He jumps and climbs like any cat
His nose and whiskers twitching
And when he sees the squirrels outside
His tail will start it's switching!

Our Tony loves to cuddle
Then curls and tucks his head
We think he dreams of catching mice
To play with in his bed!

Love Grandma Wilkie

On a cold, snowy January day, a bundle of fur was born in Saskatchewan.

His name was

TONY.

TONY

had stripes like a tiger, bright green eyes, and a letter "M" on his forehead.

This little kitten was one year old when he moved from the country farm to the city lights of Regina.

Tony moved into a house that already had two cats. These cats did not like Tony. They were mean to him and wanted to fight.

Tony was sad and very scared living with these mean cats, so he was often outside all day and night going on adventures.

TONY

loved to explore the new
neighbourhood and make
new friends.

Pouncing on flying leaves
and chasing grasshoppers
and bugs made him happy.

Tony visited one neighbour's
house all the time.

He cuddled with the family on their soft outdoor pillows and liked to sit at their red front door.

First spring came, then summer, then fall and winter. The nice family often saw little Tony sitting outside alone in the pouring rain and falling snow.

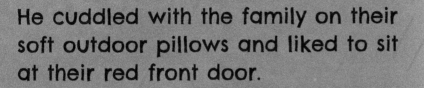

THEIR HEARTS BROKE.

The family would call outside for him—"Tony!"—welcoming him inside to warm up and keep dry.

Tony always thanked this family by purring in his distinct way. It sounded more like snoring and always made the family smile.

"That's just our **Tony**!" the family would say.

But there were dangers in this new city.

The streets had fast cars and there were animals that did not want to be friends with him.

Late one night, one of the very mean cats hurt poor Tony.

He was afraid so he hurried to the front door of the home he always visited and looked for the people he trusted.

Little Tony meowed, crying for help at the red front door.

These friends rushed him to the animal doctor.

The animal doctor cleaned his cuts, put band aids on his leg, and gave him medicine to make him feel better.

One month later in December, just before Tony's second birthday, this family adopted him.

What a beautiful Christmas they had together.

Tony was the only cat living in his new home. He now had a mom, dad, and two brothers who loved him so very much.

Tony is warm, safe, and loved in his forever home.

ADOPTED AND ADORED!

THE
END

Photography credit:
Adam Reiland Photography

ABOUT THE AUTHOR

Maureen Rose Wilkie has always been an animal lover. Her book JUST OUR TONY was inspired by her family's own adoption of an injured cat. She lives in Regina, Saskatchewan, with her family and their cat, Tony.

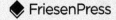 FriesenPress

One Printers Way
Altona, MB R0G 0B0
Canada

www.friesenpress.com

ISBN
978-1-03-916212-9 (Hardcover)
978-1-03-916211-2 (Paperback)
978-1-03-916213-6 (eBook)

1. JUVENILE FICTION, ANIMALS, CATS

Distributed to the trade by The Ingram Book Company

Printed in the USA
CPSIA information can be obtained
at www.ICGtesting.com
LVHW061147140124
768964LV00013B/72